AUG 1 6 19

Dreams

EZRA JACK KEATS

A Monogram Book

MACMILLAN PUBLISHING COMPANY
NEW YORK

MAXWELL MACMILLAN CANADA
TORONTO

MAXWELL MACMILLAN INTERNATIONAL
NEW YORK   OXFORD   SINGAPORE   SYDNEY

For Mitsue Ishitake,
Sachiko Saionji,
Yosuke Seki,
and my friends
of the Ohanashi Caravan

It was hot.
After supper Roberto came
to his window to talk with Amy.
"Look what I made in school today—
a paper mouse!"
"Does it do anything?" Amy asked.
Roberto thought for a while.
"I don't know," he said. Then he put
the mouse on the windowsill.

As it grew darker, the city got quieter.
"Bedtime, Roberto," called his mother.
"Bedtime for you, too,"
other mothers called.
"Good-night, Amy."
"Good-night, Roberto."
"G-o-o-o-o-d-night!" echoed the parrot.
Soon they were all in bed.

Someone began to dream.

Soon everybody was dreaming—
except one person.

Somehow Roberto just couldn't fall asleep.
It got later and later.

Finally he got up
and went to the window.
What he saw down in the street
made him gasp!

There was Archie's cat!
A big dog had chased him into a box.
The dog snarled.
"He's trapped!" thought Roberto.
"What should I do?"

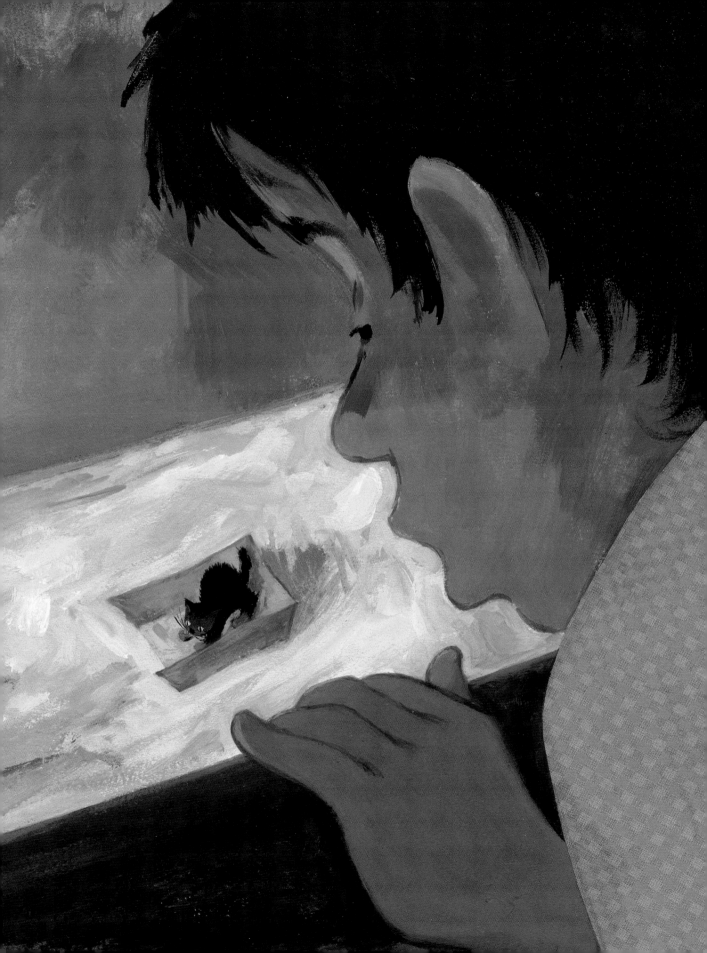

Then it happened!
His pajama sleeve
brushed the paper mouse
off the windowsill.
It sailed away from him.

Down it fell,
turning this way
and that,
casting a big shadow
on the wall.

The shadow grew bigger—
and bigger—

and BIGGER!
The dog howled and ran away.

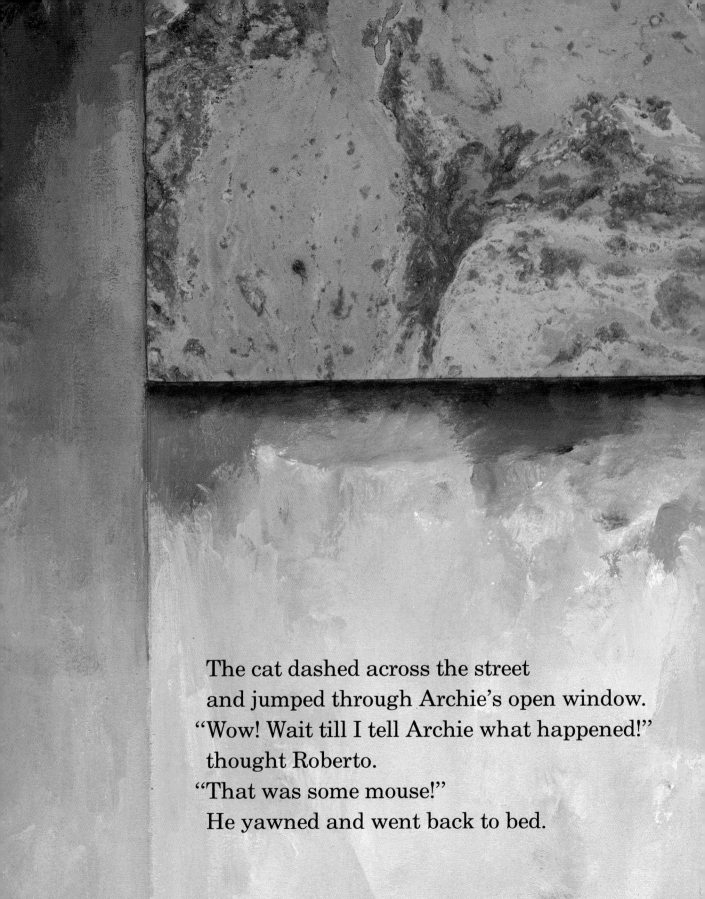

The cat dashed across the street
and jumped through Archie's open window.
"Wow! Wait till I tell Archie what happened!"
thought Roberto.
"That was some mouse!"
He yawned and went back to bed.

Morning came, and everybody
was getting up.
Except one person.

Roberto was fast asleep,
dreaming.

Macmillan Publishing Company is part of the
Maxwell Communication Group of Companies.
Macmillan Publishing Company
866 Third Avenue
New York, NY 10022
Maxwell Macmillan Canada, Inc.
1200 Eglinton Avenue East
Suite 200
Don Mills, Ontario M3C 3N1

Printed in the United States of America

10 9 8 7 6 5 4 3 2 1

The text of this book is set in 16 pt. Century Schoolbook.
The illustrations are rendered in collage and acrylics.

Library of Congress Cataloging-in-Publication Data
Keats, Ezra Jack.   Dreams.
Summary: One night while everyone is sleeping,
a little boy watches his paper mouse save a cat
from an angry dog.
I. Title.   PZ7.K2253Dr   [E]   73-15857

ISBN 0-02-749611-2 (supersedes previous ISBN)